The Bunnies' Alphabet Eggs

Story by Lisa Bassett
Pictures by Jeni Bassett

JellyBean Press
New York • Avenel, New Jersey

To Will Johnston,
who introduced me to these bunnies on a beautiful spring day.

This 1993 edition is published by JellyBean Press, a division of dilithium Press, Ltd.,
distributed by Outlet Book Company, Inc., a Random House Company,
40 Engelhard Avenue, Avenel, New Jersey 07001.

DILITHIUM is a registered trademark and
JELLYBEAN PRESS is a trademark of dilithium Press, Ltd.

Printed and bound in the United States of America

Book design: Melissa Ring • Cover design: Bill Akunevicz, Jr.
Production supervision: Roméo Enriquez • Editorial supervision: Claire Booss

Library of Congress Cataloging-in-Publication Data
Bassett, Lisa.
The bunnies' alphabet eggs / story by Lisa Bassett ; pictures by Jeni Bassett.
p. cm.
Summary: When little bunnies try to help replace his ruined eggs,
the Easter Bunny isn't sure what children will think of them.
ISBN 0-517-08153-9
[1. Easter eggs—Fiction. 2. Rabbits—Fiction. 3. Alphabet.]
I. Bassett, Jeni, ill. II. Title.
PZ7.B2933Bu 1993
[E]—dc20 92-37987
CIP
AC

8 7 6 5 4 3

The Easter Bunny looked around his burrow with pride. He had worked all year on his eggs, and they were all beautifully painted and carefully stacked on shelves and tables and armchairs. He only had a few more eggs to paint.

Those eggs can wait until tomorrow, thought the Easter Bunny with a yawn.

He crawled into bed and fell asleep with his ears flopped over his eyes. He dreamed that it was raining, and his nose was getting wet. He heard plop plop ploppity plop.

The Easter Bunny jumped out of bed, and his feet splashed in water. Water dripped on his head: drippity drippity. He looked up, and a drop of water hit him in the eye. His roof was leaking.

The Easter Bunny ran to get pans from the kitchen.
He put them under the drips. The pans filled with water
and sloshed about on the floor.

Then the Easter Bunny looked at his eggs. Water had
dripped down and washed off all the beautiful paint.
The water ran in red, pink, blue, and green puddles.

"My eggs!" cried the Easter Bunny, but then he realized that his bedroom was filling with water. "Oh dear, I wish I knew how to swim!" he said, as the bed began to float. He pulled himself up on the bed, as it floated into the living room. Then it floated into the kitchen. He grabbed a pan from a shelf in the kitchen and used it to paddle to the front door.

His bed bumped out the door and into the sunshine.

"It's not raining!" said the Easter Bunny, blinking his eyes and twitching his nose. "Where is that water coming from? And my eggs! What am I going to do?"

Suddenly he heard whistling. He turned around and saw Mr. Rabbit, in dungarees, watering the ground over his burrow. The ground was dug up into neat little rows.

"What are you doing?" cried the Easter Bunny, untangling himself from the sopping sheets.

"I'm watering this vegetable garden I just planted,"

said Mr. Rabbit cheerfully. "But the ground soaks up the water as fast as fast! These little seeds must be thirsty!"

"Th-th-thirsty!" cried the Easter Bunny. "You planted your garden right over my burrow. The water is running into my house! And my eggs! My beautiful eggs are ruined and tomorrow is Easter."

"Oowee!" said Mr. Rabbit. "I didn't know your house was here."

"What am I going to do?" The Easter Bunny pulled on his ears. "I can't possibly paint all of these eggs by tomorrow."

Mr. Rabbit twitched his whiskers. "Well, I have an idea," he said. "My children could help you."

"Your children?" the Easter Bunny frowned. "How many children?"

"I have ten children," said Mr. Rabbit proudly. "They could paint all the eggs you need."

"I don't know," said the Easter Bunny, shaking his head. "But, oh! I don't have a choice. I must get my eggs ready! All right. Send over your children."

Mr. Rabbit disappeared and the Easter Bunny went into his burrow. The floor was muddy and all his eggs were washed white.

Before long, ten little bunnies arrived to help. The Easter Bunny began to show them how he painted eggs. He twirled an egg on one paw, where it spun round. With a brush in the other paw, he painted stripes and dots and diamonds. The ten little bunnies gasped.

"Let me try," cried Basil, the largest of the little bunnies. He tried to twirl an egg, but before he could get his brush ready the egg fell on the floor and cracked.

"No, no!" said the Easter Bunny. "Oh my! You little bunnies will have to paint the eggs another way." The little bunnies grabbed brushes and pots of paint.

"What will you paint on the eggs?" asked the Easter Bunny anxiously. "Do you know how to make designs?"

"We know how to make our letters!" cried the bunnies. "We can draw the alphabet!"

"Well, then, put one letter on each egg," said the Easter Bunny, throwing up his paws.

Basil painted eggs with I and J and K.   Rosemary

painted eggs with N and O and P.   All the little bunnies

made different letters as they dabbed and sloshed and spattered.

By sunset, all of the Easter Bunny's eggs were painted and tucked gently into baskets. The little bunnies went skipping home, but the Easter Bunny sat in his armchair frowning.

"Oh, what will the village children think when they
find these eggs? They will miss my beautiful eggs. Oh,
oh!" He pulled his whiskers and frowned even more.
That night he could hardly sleep, and when he woke up,
he had a headache. But he knew he had to hide the
eggs.

He went to the village and hid the eggs in bushes and behind trees. For the first time, he hoped that no one would find them, because he was ashamed of them. But before the Easter Bunny could tiptoe away, he heard children coming out of their houses. The Easter Bunny crept behind a tree trunk. They will be so unhappy when they see those eggs, he thought.

Suddenly he heard shouts from the village children. "Oh dear, oh dear," said the Easter Bunny. He wanted to run away. But he listened to the shouts.

The children did not sound unhappy. They sounded happy. The Easter Bunny tiptoed closer to hear what the children said.

"Look," cried one. "I can spell F-O-O-T with my eggs."

"And I can spell S-K-Y" said another.

"I can spell more words than you! I found more eggs!" The children were laughing.

The Easter Bunny hopped home. He flopped into his damp armchair. "The children like the eggs," he said to himself over and over again, in amazement.

Just then he heard a knock on his door. He looked up and saw the ten little bunnies crowded in the doorway.

"Look," said Basil. He twirled an egg and caught it just before it fell. "I know I can get better," he said.

"Basil, you don't need to paint eggs the way I do,"

said the Easter Bunny. "You have your own way."

"But we were wondering if we could help you paint your eggs for next year. We like helping you."

The Easter Bunny smiled for the first time that day. "Basil, I could not do it without you!" said the Easter Bunny, and he gave each of the little bunnies a big Easter hug.